No Lex 12-12

Governor
Readin

RACE CAR LEGENDS

The Allisons
Mario Andretti
Crashes & Collisions
Drag Racing
Dale Earnhardt
Famous Finishes
A.J. Foyt
Formula One Racing
Jeff Gordon
The Jarretts
The Labontes
The Making of a Race Car
Monster Trucks & Tractors
Motorcycles
Richard Petty
The Pit Crew
The Unsers
Rusty Wallace
Women in Racing

CHELSEA HOUSE PUBLISHERS

RACE CAR LEGENDS

JEFF GORDON

Richard Brinster

CHELSEA HOUSE PUBLISHERS
Philadelphia

Produced by Daniel Bial and Associates
New York, New York

Picture research by Alan Gottlieb
Cover design by Takeshi Takahashi
Cover photo credit: AP/Wide World Photo

3 5 7 9 8 6 4

Library of Congress Cataloging-in-Publication Data

Brinster, Richard.
    Jeff Gordon / Richard Brinster;
      p.   cm. — (Race car legends)
    Includes bibiliographical references and index.
    ISBN 0-7910-4430-0
    1. Gordon, Jeff, 1971- —Juvenile literature. 2. Automobile racing
drivers—United States—Biography—Juvenile literature. I. Title. II. Series.
GV1032.G67875 1997
796.72'092—dc21
[B]   97-5614
                                                                                   CIP
                                                                                    AC

CONTENTS

THE DRIVE TO WIN

What's the most popular spectator sport in the United States? It's not baseball, football, basketball, or even horse racing. America's favorite sport is automobile racing.

To the outsider, it looks simple. You get in your car, keep the accelerator depressed as you hurtle around the track, expect your crew to keep the car in perfect condition, and try not to go deaf as you weave your machine through traffic toward the checkered flag. But in actuality, it's not at all easy. Just as baseball isn't simply a matter of hitting the ball, so racing is full of subtleties.

What does it take to be a world-class race car driver? The more you know about the lives of the greats, the more it becomes clear that each successful driver is an extraordinary athlete gifted with unusual vision, coordination, and the will to win. The concentration necessary to send a car speeding around a track at 200 miles per hour for hour after hour, when a momentary lapse can cause instant death for him and any unfortunate driver near him, is phenomenal. Any driver worth his salt must be strong, self-confident, resilient, and willing to take risks in order to have an opportunity to win.

In addition, the top drivers have to be good businessmen and know how to put together a winning team. They have to find sponsors to put them in competitive cars. They rely on a pit crew to make sure that their car is always in peak performance condition. And they have to be mentally prepared each race day to take into consideration a host of factors: weather, the other racers, the condition of the track, and how their car is responding on that day. Without everything right, a driver won't stand a chance of winning.

The drivers in the Race Car Legends series grew up around race cars. The fathers of Richard Petty and Dale Earnhardt were very successful race car drivers themselves. A. J. Foyt's father was a part-time racer and a full-time mechanic; the Allisons and Unsers are an extended family of racers. Only Mario Andretti's father disapproved of his son's racing. Yet Mario and his twin brother Aldo devoted themselves to racing at a young age.

Despite the knowledge and connection a family can provide, few of the legendary racers portrayed in this series met with immediate success. They needed to prove themselves in sprint cars or midget cars before they were allowed to get behind the wheel of a contending stock car or a phenomenally expensive Indy car. They needed to be tested in the tough races on the hardscrabble tracks before they learned enough to handle the race situations at Daytona or the Brickyard. They needed to learn how to get the most out of whatever vehicle they were piloting, including knowing how to fix an engine in the wee hours of the night before a big race.

A driver also has to learn to face adversity, because crashes often take the lives of friends or relatives. Indeed, every driver has been lucky at one point or another to survive a scare or a bad accident. "We've had our tragedies, but what family hasn't?" remarked the mother of Al and Bobby Unser. "I don't blame racing. I love racing as our whole family has."

What each driver has proved is that success in this most grueling sport takes commitment. Walter Payton, the great football running back, and Paul Newman, star of many blockbuster movies, have both taken up racing—and proved they have some talent behind the wheel. Still, it's evident that neither has been able to provide the devotion it takes to be successful at the highest levels.

To be a great driver, racing has to be in your blood.

1

A STAR IS BORN

Jeff Gordon, known to racing fans as "The Kid," saw the white flag and knew he was about to drive the toughest lap of his life. But thanks to some great pit work, there was nothing left to beat except his own emotions.

"I was trying not to hit the wall from all the tears that were coming down my face," The Kid was to say later.

He drove low into the first turn, eased up the banking and headed down the long backstretch. He repeated the pattern entering the third turn and exited the fourth as Doyle Ford got ready with the checkered flag. Seconds later, Ford waved the banner and Jeff Gordon had won the Coca-Cola 600, his first Winston Cup race.

On May 29, 1994, a new star was born. "If there's a feeling higher than this, I don't know what it is," Gordon said in the winner's circle that Sunday afternoon at Charlotte Motor Speedway. "This absolutely is the greatest moment of

Jeff Gordon, in his number 24 car, blazes to victory in the 1994 running of the Coca Cola 600.

my life. This is a memory and feeling I'll never forget."

As it would come to pass, Gordon was only a year away from greatness. By the end of the next season, the National Association for Stock Car Auto Racing (NASCAR) would be crowning a new Winston Cup champion.

At 22, he was Rookie of the Year. Before reaching 23, he became the youngest first-time winner on the circuit. Dale Earnhardt and Darrell Waltrip—the biggest established stars on the circuit and who have combined to win over 150 races—were much older when they won their first Winston Cup races. After just three years on the circuit, Jeff Gordon would look up to find only 13 drivers who made more money in their NASCAR careers. And, as he was to prove that Memorial Day weekend in the deep South, Gordon also had a nose for business.

His prize for winning the Coca-Cola 600 was $196,500. Shortly after the race, Gordon was talking with track owner Bruton Smith. Gordon joked that the payoff should have been a nice, round number.

Smith reached into his pocket and pulled out a wad of money. He counted off 35 $100 bills and handed them to Gordon. The Kid's winnings were now a "round" $200,000.

But The Kid did not keep a dime of his winnings. The money went right to crew chief Ray Evernham. "He's the one who made this happen," Gordon said.

Evernham had provided Gordon with a terrific strategy—and a fast car.

From the moment he drove his Chevrolet Lumina onto the 1.5-mile Charlotte track, Gordon had a special feeling. Joe Nemechek had

posted the fastest qualifying speed—180.252 miles per hour fifteen minutes before a curious Gordon took his qualifying run.

"You don't know if you've got a car capable of going for the pole until you drop that thing down into the first corner," he said.

After streaking through the dogleg where the start-finish line is located, Gordon reached the short straight just before the first high-banked turn. In matter of seconds he knew. "I was smiling all the way down the backstretch," he said.

He turned in the fastest time, clocking an average speed 181.439 miles per hour to win the pole (the inside position in the front row that affords the driver an immediate lead at the start of the race). In doing so, he broke a stranglehold that Ford drivers had enjoyed; Thunderbirds had started from the pole position in the previous 10 races. But winning the pole was a long way from winning the race. But Gordon had already

In his final pitstop of the race, Gordon opted to only have two tires changed—and the time saved allowed him to win.

known success at Charlotte. In years past, Gordon had finished second in the Coca-Cola 600, then sat on the pole for the fall race at Charlotte in 1993.

Gordon had won a qualifying race a week earlier at Charlotte. He had also driven his Chevy in the Winston Select, a rich non-points race held a week before the Coca-Cola 600. Gordon's car was banged around a lot as he finished 14th in the 20-car field.

"They pretty much had to put a new nose on it, front fenders, and a right side," he said of his crew. "They worked until three in the morning some mornings just to get it ready."

"We're real happy to be the first Chevrolet on the pole this year, but also the first Chevrolet on Goodyears on the pole," Gordon said. He was referring obliquely to the most famous Chevrolet driver also in the race, Dale Earnhart, and to a recently brewing tire rivalry. Hoosier, an Indiana-based tire company, had already persuaded Geoff Bodine and Nemechek to use their tires—and had tried to coax Gordon to join their ranks.

Earnhardt and Sterling Marlin arrived at Charlotte knowing a victory by either, combined with one in the Southern 500 on Labor Day weekend, would be worth $1 million. Marlin had won the Daytona 500 and Earnhardt the Winston Select 500. Any driver to win three of the four events in the same season gets a $1 million bonus. In 1985, Bill Elliott became the first—and so far only—driver ever to cash the big check.

The race was a tight one all the way. With over 300 of the 400 laps down, a caution flag came out, and all the leaders used this opportunity to head for the pits.

Dale Jarrett went in first but came out second, a victim of quick work by Rusty Wallace's pit crew—widely regarded as the best in the business. When the race went back to green on lap 324, Wallace steadily pulled away from the lead pack.

Jarrett, meantime, had his hands full with Bodine and Gordon. While they battled it out for second, Wallace built his edge to about two seconds.

Bodine eventually worked his way to second, then began to slowly track down Wallace. At that point, there were 30 laps left, and it was apparent nobody could go all the way on fuel and everyone's tires were becoming very worn.

Wallace was the first to come in, on lap 379. As usual, he had by far the best time among the drivers who made four-tire stops. While all the leaders pitted for four tires and fuel, Ray Evernham had Gordon remain on the track. Evernham remembered a trick the great Richard Petty used several times, including once to win the 1981 Daytona 500.

Bruton Smith helped Gordon hold his trophy after the race—and also rounded Gordon's winnings up to an even $200,000.

When Gordon came in for his last pit stop, Evernham took a big gamble, giving him fuel and just two tires. If either of the two worn tires blew, not only would Gordon lose, he might also crash.

Gordon charged out of the pits and found himself in first place, 250 yards ahead of Wallace. His tires held up fine and all Gordon had to do was dodge traffic for the final nine laps. After 600 miles spread over 4 hours, 18 minutes, 10 seconds, The Kid won by 3.91 seconds.

That margin of victory would definitely have been wiped out had Gordon stayed to get all new tires in his last pit stop.

"It was a chancy move to put just two tires on," Wallace said later. "We really had them beat bad today. It was almost disgusting how bad we had them beat. I never thought he'd try two tires, and I never thought it would work."

"I'd have to say Gordon outfoxed everybody tonight," said Jarrett, who finished fourth.

Wallace, figuring all the drivers would follow his lead, wasn't sure whether to be upset or embarrassed by what had happened. He led for 187 of the 400 laps, easily dominating the race.

"In hindsight, we should have changed two and we would have won by a ton," he said. "But it was a pretty savvy move on their part. They did a good job."

Bodine, Hoosier's point man throughout the season, wound up third. When asked about Gordon, he just shook his head and said: "I can't believe it."

True to his character, Gordon wanted no credit. "I didn't know what they were going to do until they told me to leave the pits," he said of the strategy.

In just his 42nd start, The Kid was a winner of one the most coveted races in the sport.

"I had nothing to do with it," Gordon said of the crucial call.

"It's an incredible feeling to get this far in your career. It's everything you've ever worked for. I've won a lot of races, but none of them have felt like this," he said, once again fighting back the tears.

2

THE KID EMERGES

Jeff Gordon was born August 4, 1971, in Vallejo, California, a mile or so from the Mare Island Naval Shipyard on the eastern shore of San Pablo Bay, about 25 miles from San Francisco.

By the time Jeff was four, he was involved in bicycle motocross racing, and his mother was worried. "At BMX events, they were hauling kids away in ambulances at the time," Carol Bickford said. She put a stop to his racing, but her husband, Jeff's stepfather, had other ideas.

John Bickford, an auto parts manufacturer and a racing devotee, bought Jeff a quarter midget, a tiny racing machine with a 2.85-horse-power engine. "He bought a black one for me and a pink one for my sister, Kim," Gordon recalled. "I was 4, and she was 8." Upset at first, Mrs. Bickford soon realized "it was a lot safer than the bikes." Still, Gordon wasn't allowed to compete until he was 5, so he spent a year careening around a parking lot.

In 1991, Jeff Gordon drove this car on the Busch Grand National circuit.

Soon Gordon could be seen in competition. An early family home movie shows a contest with little boys calmly circling a small racing surface, keeping their lines and following one another.

Suddenly, into the right corner of the screen, comes one vehicle going considerably faster than the others. The leader gets a bit wide on a corner, leaving an opening on the inside.

There isn't enough room to get through. But that doesn't bother the little boy with the determined look on his face. Jeff Gordon dives to the inside, runs over the tire of the leader, drives away and leaves the rest of the field in his wake.

By the time he was eight, Jeff Gordon won his first national championship in quarter midgets. A year later, he would be beating boys nearly twice his age in go-karts.

Bickford realized Jeff was an unusual talent, and they soon began a program designed to carry the young charger to greatness in racing. They ran 52 weeks each year, and practiced two or three times per week.

"We were the Roger Penske of quarter midgets," Bickford told *Sports Illustrated*, referring to the great Indy car owner.

When Jeff moved up to the 10-horsepower go-karts, parents of the other racers figured he was lying about his age and really was about 20 but on the smallish side.

That much hasn't changed. The 5'7", 160-pound Gordon now has the appearance of a high school kid who sneaked into the NASCAR garage area disguised as a driver, who may be caught at any minute.

"Nobody wanted to race us," Bickford said. "Those kids were 13 to 17, and we were killing them. We then moved up to superstock light.

Now we were running against guys 17 and older. And those guys were going, 'There's no damn nine-year-old kid gonna run with us! Get outta here.' "

Jeff returned to quarter midgets, won a second national title at 10, but felt trapped. By the time he was 12, Jeff Gordon had nothing left to accomplish at the grass roots level of racing.

He was ready to move up, but the bigger cars could not be driven most places by someone his age. In the Midwest, however, Bickford discovered a circuit where their was no minimum age requirement.

"Nobody was fool enough to drive that young," Gordon said. "So they didn't think they needed an age rule."

So, the family moved to Pittsboro, Indiana, 20 miles from the state capital and a hallowed piece of ground off West 16th Street known as the Indianapolis Motor Speedway.

Each year, for a few hours on a Sunday afternoon on Memorial Day weekend, this huge arena holds the attention of auto racing fans around the globe. They run the Indianapolis 500, the world's most famous race. But it is more than just a race. It is one of the great annual sporting events in the United States. Among one-day events, only the Super Bowl, and perhaps the Kentucky Derby, get more attention. Neither, however, draws crowds in excess of 400,000.

None of this can be lost on a kid growing up just down the road driving midgets and sprint cars. They are the proving ground for the lucky few who one day graduate to big leagues of open-wheel racing — the Indy cars.

Jeff Gordon was no different than most of the other local kids interested in racing. Perhaps the

Gordon learned how to pilot stock cars by attending the driving school of NASCAR Hall of Famer Buck Baker.

only thing that set him apart from them was his early start.

At 13, Jeff went to war in a $25,000 sprint car John Bickford built for him. Behind the wheel of one of those 650-horsepower monsters, Gordon was now light years removed from the lawnmower-type engines he used to race to his early victories.

At 14, he was driving sprint cars at places like Winchester, the Indiana short track whose fast and high-banked layout often is featured on ESPN's racing series. The ultra-fast, half-mile oval is exciting and sometimes frightening to watch — particularly from an in-car camera.

He drove on the winter circuit in Florida in 1985, and settled in after the family's move to Indiana in 1986 to become the young terror of tracks there and in Ohio and Illinois.

Before he was old enough to get an Indiana driver's license, he had won three sprint races against the best competition in the Midwest. When Gordon graduated from high school, he had to decide if he wanted to go to college or race. It was a serious decision. "I started to look at racing as a job," said Gordon after he made his choice. "The night I graduated from high school, I finished fourth in a sprint-car race at Bloomington, Indiana."

At 18, Gordon was driving 1,300-pound, 815-horsepower sprint cars. These fast, light vehicles whiz around high-banked circuits and can be highly dangerous, especially when handled by less-than-expert drivers. In comparison, Winston Cup cars are heavier, weighing 3,400 pounds, and less powerful, developing about 700 horsepower, than the midgets run on the United States Auto Club circuit. Gordon won the USAC midgets championship that season.

Two years later, his parents advised Jeff to look into stock cars. He went south, to the racing school operated by NASCAR Hall of Famer Buck Baker at Rockingham, North Carolina.

"That first day, the first time I got in . . . I said 'This is it.' It felt big and heavy," Gordon recalled. "It felt very fast, but very smooth. I loved it."

By 1991, there was little doubt Gordon was well on his way to the top of his profession. He drove on the NASCAR's Busch Grand National tour, just a level below the heralded Winston Cup division.

Driving for owner Bill Davis, Gordon continued his run of early dominance, winning the Busch series Rookie of the Year award. At the same time, he won USAC's Silver Crown series for open-wheel cars.

The next season, Jeff was noticed by Rick Hendrick, the Charlotte-based auto dealership giant who also owns a stable of Winston Cup cars.

On a Saturday in March 1992, Hendrick was in a luxury box watching a Busch race in Atlanta. As often is the case, some Winston Cup stars ran the race to become better prepared for their featured event the next afternoon on the 1.522-mile track.

Gordon battled veterans Dale Earnhardt and Harry Gant. Hendrick kept an eye on the unknown challenger with the dangerous chas-

By the time he was 20, Gordon had already won more than 500 races.

sis setup. Gordon was loose and fast through the corners, running what is known in the business as the ragged edge — going as fast as one can up to the point of losing control.

"I saw [him] go into the turn in three and four and he was so loose. He was really hazing his tires," Hendrick remembered. "I said, 'Watch this guy bust his butt.' But he kept racing like that lap after lap after lap."

The ragged edge is generally negotiated without problems only by the greats of the sport and some of its most talented veterans. Most young drivers either don't have the equipment, the knowledge, or the courage to pull it off. No matter how impressive they appear, young drivers eventually sway the chassis too much and spin out, often putting themselves into a wall and getting hurt. Gordon didn't do it that afternoon, nor has he ever had a serious crash. The most devastating injury of his life came when he fell and broke his nose as a five-year-old.

"Dale Earnhardt and Harry Gant were leading, and this white car was right up on them," Hendrick recalled. "I told the people with me, 'You just can't drive a car that loose.'" But Gordon held on to win his first NASCAR-sanctioned victory.

"I asked who the driver was. Somebody said, 'That's that kid Gordon.'"

Hendrick was immediately reminded of the prodigy of his multi-car operation of the 1980s. "I said, 'It's too bad he's got a contract because I see a lot of Tim Richmond in him, hanging his car out there like that lap after lap after lap.' His roommate said, 'He doesn't have a contract.' Two days later, he did."

In his first meeting with Gordon, Hendrick saw something he had not expected. "I was almost in a daze," he said. "Jeff had it all. It was just scary. He's good looking, and I couldn't believe how well he handled himself at age 20. What I found was a mature, young guy who was kind of humble, a little bit bashful—a sponsor's dream."

By the time he reached his twentieth birthday, Gordon had posted more than 500 short track victories. He moved to stocks in 1991, winning the Grand National rookie title. The next year, he won three Busch races and a series-record 11 poles and earned his Winston Cup shot from Hendrick.

With NASCAR's rapid expansion in the late 1980s and early 1990s from a Southeast regional sport to one of truly national appeal—with each race televised—a new wave or drivers emerged.

There was the late Alan Kulwicki, who came out of Wisconsin to challenge the Good Ol' Boys and eventually win the Winston Cup championship. Richmond was from Ohio. Ernie Irvan, also a transplanted Californian, was the sport's next star.

Finally, there was The Kid, from California by way of Indiana.

3

THE PRODIGY

By the end of 1992, after Gordon had won 11 Busch poles and three races, there were no mountains left to climb in stock cars except one —the Mount Everest of the sport—the Winston Cup circuit.

Although he had plans for Gordon for 1993, Hendrick put The Kid behind the wheel for the 1992 fall race in Atlanta, Georgia. He qualified 21st—no easy feat for a first-timer in the world of the Earnhardts and Wallaces—in the Hooters 500.

Gordon finished 31st, collecting $6,285. His performance did little to attract the attention of reporters, who may have figured he was just another young also-ran thrown into a season-ending race to see how he could do against the

In 1993, Dale Earnhardt and Jeff Gordon watched the qualifying at the Daytona Speedway. Earnhardt, the greatest racer of his time, lost the lead for the Daytona 500 on the last lap—for the second time in his career. That year, Jeff made history by being the youngest driver ever to win a Daytona qualifier.

big boys. However, his next competitive appearance was something not to be forgotten on the circuit.

Gordon opened the 1993 season with a stunning victory in one of the qualifying races for the Daytona 500. At 21, he had mastered the Daytona International Speedway, the graveyard of hopes for many a driver with far more experience.

Daytona is billed the World Center of Speed. In baseball, the ultimate event of the season is the World Series. In football, it is the Super Bowl. In hockey, it is the Stanley Cup. All of these are held at the end of the season. In stock-car racing, however, the biggest event of the year starts the season off. Every February, all the greats come to Florida to test themselves and see if they can put their names in the record books. Richard Petty has—he won here seven times in his illustrious career. Dale Earnhardt also has—if only because he has yet to win the Daytona 500.

In 1993, Jeff Gordon put his name in the record books by becoming the youngest driver ever to win a Daytona qualifier. He erased the mark set by Johnny Rutherford, who later went on to win three Indy 500s. Rutherford's mark had stood for three decades.

In 1993, Gordon entered the big-time world of Winston Cup racing. A "rookie stripe" was placed on the rear fender of his car to alert other drivers of his supposed lack of experience.

With Bobby Labonte and Kenny Wallace among those first joining the tour, the competition for 1993 Rookie-of-the-Year honors figured to be fierce.

It wasn't.

Gordon opened the season with a fifth-place finish at Daytona, a staggering achievement for anyone so young and proof that his qualifying race victory three days earlier was not a fluke.

Although he won no major races, Gordon finished in the top five seven times and 11 times in the top ten. That was good enough for him to be named rookie of the year on the Winston Cup circuit. The 22-year-old was pleased, but in typical fashion, said he could have done better. "I looked at this year as a learning experience and as a chance to do some pretty good things," he said in New York where collected a $25,000 check for being named the top rookie in the series.

"We had a good year," he said. "I learned a lot and I had the opportunity to race with the best drivers in the world."

He also won a decent amount of prize money: $725,163 to be exact. Of course, all the money goes first to the owner who uses it to defray the costs of maintaining the car and hiring the crew. But there was some disappointment in his heart as Gordon accepted the applause and the money. Late in the season, he had been among the top points winners of all Winston Cup racers, but had fallen out of the top ten with only a few races left.

"I felt like we were awful close to a win a few times," Gordon said. "I just thought we'd win a race and one of our goals was to finish in the top 10 in the points. You like to reach your goals."

One goal he and crew chief Ray Evernham did reach was winning a pole, a feat they accomplished at Charlotte in October. It was to put them in the rich Busch Clash the following February at Daytona.

"That pole was a big thing for our team," Gordon said. "It made us all feel like we were on the right track, going in the right direction. I just wish we could have won a race, too."

Soon, the comparisons began. Could he be as good as Earnhardt? How about Davey Allison, who inherited the legacy of Richmond, only to be killed in a 1993 helicopter crash at Talladega? How good was he, really?

The Kid didn't have to answer that question. Earnhardt, who had taken a liking to Gordon early on, did it for him. "His age doesn't really have anything to do with it," Earnhardt said. "That Gordon boy is a very good driver.

"I have no problem racing with him anywhere on any track," the man known as the Terminator continued. "He's probably going to win a lot of races and some championships."

Considering that there are close to 40 well-equipped cars driven by as many skilled racers, that sound like some longshot prediction. But Earnhardt know talent when he sees is. He liked very much what he saw in Gordon, although even he probably could not have figured it would happen as fast as it did.

Gordon treated all his new-found fame in modest fashion. "Winning Rookie of the Year was a goal we had all season long and we're happy about that," he said. "But there was some really great competition from Bobby and Kenny. I'd like to think all three of us have a pretty good future in Winston Cup racing."

Actually, Bobby Labonte and Kenny Wallace had not given Gordon much competition on the tracks. But Gordon was right about their futures. Labonte was to become a star two years later, and although Wallace has yet to win a Winston Cup event, he is considered one of the better young drivers in the series.

Comparisons don't sit well with Evernham, himself a former terror in the modified division in his native New Jersey.

"I don't think it's fair to compare great drivers against each other," Evernham said. "No one is great across the board, except maybe Dale Earnhardt. But there's only one of him.

"Jeff doesn't like to be compared to other drivers," Evernham continued. "He doesn't like to be compared to Richard Petty or Davey Allison. It's not fair to Jeff or those guys. He's trying to be as humble as he can. He'll tell you he doesn't have a God-given talent. He'll tell you he's just driven race cars all his life."

Still, The Kid can't escape those comparisons. Early success has its price. How Gordon was to survive it would be the key to his future.

At the 1993 Pepsi 400, Jimmy Hensley (center) lost control of his car directly in front of Jeff Gordon (right). Neither driver was seriously injured in the crash.

The fierceness of the competition hasn't escaped him. "I knew there would be a lot of learn when I got to Winston Cup," he said. "But the competition really is incredible. You can do everything right and still wind up fifth or sixth or 12th because that many other guys are having a great race. But we do have a great owner and a great race team and our goals are to be competitive, win some races next season and eventually win the championship."

At the time, such talk may have seemed like wishful thinking. It wasn't. "I can't wait for next season to get started," he said.

The start of the next season brought an unusual revelation. Gordon announced he was engaged to be married to Brooke Sealy. Sealy, nearly a year older than Gordon, was winner of the Miss Winston beauty pageant in 1993. Her role as Miss Winston was to smile in the winner's circle and plant a kiss on the cheek of the victorious driver. According to the rules of the contest, she was not allowed to date any drivers.

Gordon met Sealy after his victory in the 1993 Daytona qualifier. Gordon took one look at the stunning brunette and had a feeling this was the woman of his future. Jeff wasted no time in the winner's circle that February afternoon and immediately asked her to lunch. Then the deception began. They spent stolen moments during 1993 seeing each other when and where they could.

"Everybody knows you can't date Miss Winston, and I did," he was later to confess. "Hiding her for so long was difficult."

Each would show up at racing festivities without an escort and never seemed to have a date. People in the sport began to wonder how two people so young and attractive could be loners.

"Earnhardt asked if I was gay," Gordon joked with a reporter. "I am now a master at sneaking in and out of hotels."

There were the restaurant rendezvous and the other deceptions. Once, when they planned to take the same flight, Darrell Waltrip's crew showed up just before Jeff and Brooke were to board their plane.

Brooke left the gate area and hid out until everybody was gone. She caught a flight two hours later.

She proved to be more than a pretty face and a stabilizing influence on the young star. Brooke became Jeff's good-luck charm. "Ever since Brooke and I have been able to tell people we were dating, and then tell them we were married, it seems my luck has changed.

Jeff Gordon's crew pushes his car back to the garage after rain canceled a day of qualifying at the Charlotte Motor Speedway.

"My luck never was the same until I could tell everybody about our relationship," Gordon continued. "Now, I'm very happy at the racetrack and I'm very happy away from the racetrack. It helps me stay focused. . . . Keep Brooke happy, because she makes me happy. When she makes me happy, I drive better."

The night before the running of the Busch Clash at Daytona, Gordon proposed to Brooke. He had brought a ring to the French restaurant and was waiting for the right moment to pop the question. Just as he was getting ready, he noticed "some folk from Unocal having their function." Not wanting to propose while racing people were watching, he delayed leaving the restaurant, going to the bathroom several times, and ordering dessert, something he ordinarily never does. Finally, the right moment came. Jeff proposed, Brooke accepted and cried. It has not been revealed whether Jeff ate his dessert after the engagement dinner in Daytona Beach. But it didn't bother him the next day. He went out and won the Busch Clash. Later, he won twice in the span of a week at Charlotte. The first victory didn't count in the standings because it came in the Winston Select Open. But the second—officially the first of his Winston Cup career—began a run whose end appears nowhere in sight.

On November 26, 1994, Jeff and Brooke married; *Carolina Bride* magazine printed a great story about their wedding. The Gordons then settled down in a house on the shore of Lake Norman, a large body of water outside Charlotte nicknamed Lake Speed because so many race drivers live there.

After a honeymoon in St. Martin, the Gordons flew to New York for the NASCAR awards banquet. As the eighth-place finisher in the Winston Cup race, Jeff got to collect $7,500 and make a speech. In it, he paid tribute to Brooke.

"It was really fun for me because now I'm married, I get to say wife," Jeff said. "For so long it's like girlfriend, fiancée. And I was finally able to say 'My beautiful wife.' So that was a perfect place to do it at, really the first time."

Like their engagement dinner, Brooke had no idea what Jeff would say. She urged him to write a speech or at least some notes. He did neither, nor did he know what he would say. It just came out.

"Here I was thinking all the people that were special to me in racing and she plays a major role in being very special on and off the race track," Gordon said.

By the time the 1994 season was put in the record book, Gordon would win $1,779,523. He would have the kind of season drivers with a two decades of experience could only dream about. There would be two wins, one second, one third, two fourths, a fifth, and seven more top-10 finishes.

For most, it would be considered a career year. But Gordon was sure his future was still brighter than his past.

"The sky's the limit," Hendrick said before Gordon had finished posting his gaudy numbers. "The first time I saw him race, I didn't even know the name but I knew he was something special."

But Dale Jarrett pretty much summed it up.

"It should be illegal to be that young, that good looking, and that talented," he said.

Start of First Brickyard 400 - 94' which Jeff won

Earnhardt   Must.   Martin

THE BRICKYARD

Two months after his triumph in the big race at Charlotte, Jeff Gordon was still looking for his second victory. The next big race on the circuit brought him to his old stomping grounds, Indianapolis.

The Indianapolis Motor Speedway was hosting a stock car race. According to tradition, this was unthinkable. The stocks cars had their cherished Daytona 500 and the open-wheel machines had their beloved Indianapolis 500. Case closed.

But the business end of auto racing finally outran its tradition, and 85 years after it was built, Indy became the scene of a battle among Chevrolets, Fords, and Pontiacs.

Right track—wrong cars? In 1994, for the first time, stock cars engaged in a major race at the Indianapolis Motor Speedway. Dale Earnhardt (left front) and Rick Mast (right front) started off in front of the pack, but the eventual winner was the hometown boy, Jeff Gordon, whose car can be seen behind Mast's.

A win here would provide more than recognition among stock car fans. History was to be made that first Saturday in August 1994. Someone would get his name on a trophy as the winner of the inaugural Brickyard 400.

This one would be the most-talked-about, most-well-attended and richest and most curious stock car race in history. The Indianapolis track seats more than 250,000. Daytona International Speedway, limited by outside factors, seats less than half that number. Organizers closed the infield, leading some people to speculate that the speedway didn't to be embarrassed by having the largest crowd ever at the home of the Indianapolis 500 show up for a stock-car race.

Given the well-established loyalty of the old fans, the great growth of the sport, and the novelty of the first stock car race, some said Indy could have sold a half-million tickets. Still, the $3.2 million purse surpassed the record $2.75 million payout of the Daytona 500. So NASCAR's richest race was no longer the Daytona 500.

But none of that was of any interest to the other drivers who sought to make the 43-car field for the first Brickyard 400. Jeff Gordon had another reason not to care about the dollars. His place in history was more important.

"I lived about 15 or 20 miles from here out in Hendricks County. I went to Tri-West High School and graduated from there," Gordon said of his roots. "To make history here in NASCAR is more than a dream come true. This is one of the greatest things I've ever done in my life. To see all these fans when you come driving down that front straightaway is just the greatest thrill ever."

Gordon relies on his crew as he pulls in for a pitstop at the Brickyard 400.

And this was still days before practice began.

"If it was just another race, everybody wouldn't have been up here testing so much," he said. "When we drive out there for the first time, that's when the chills will start going up my spine."

For the crowd, it was to be a little different until they realized what they were seeing. Then a quiet audience warmed to the show on that warm Saturday afternoon.

Gordon, who that day was to be "discovered" by millions, staged a great battle with Ernie Irvan. Much of the final 20 laps was an all-out duel between The Kid and a driver once called Swervin' Irvan because he kept wrecking fields. Now, Irvan was leading in the points race and just as eager as the young Hoosier to make history.

The 1994 Brickyard 400 came down to an exciting duel between Ernie Irvan and Jeff Gordon.

"It got very exciting the last 20 or 30 laps," Gordon recalled. "I didn't know what was going to happen."

Each time they traded leads, the car in front would begin getting loose as the trailing car took air off its rear spoiler. Less downforce means a fast but slippery ride.

"When I was leading, he could get right up on me and loosen me up and I'd have to let him go by," Gordon said. "But the thing was, I could do the same thing again. I could get right up on him and loosen him up."

He did just that, all the time hoping he could somehow get away from Irvan.

"Ernie and I, man, we had one heck of a race. The last guy I wanted to race at the end was Ernie. He's so tough."

Finally, Gordon showed wisdom beyond his years.

"We were just counting down the laps, because it wasn't doing me any good to be in front of him. But I thought maybe I could help wear his tires out a little bit and wait there towards the end and get a run on him."

As the laps wound down, crew chief Ray Evernham was trying to help Gordon with his strategy. "The Kid's going to take one more shot at him, I hope."

Gordon did just that, moving alongside Irvan on the backstretch on lap 156. Both cars stayed side by side until Irvan slowed suddenly, his right front tire cut and his hopes of victory gone.

"With four laps to go, five maybe, I drove as hard as I could in on him to try to get him loose going into the corner, not to spin him out or anything," Gordon said. "Then, all of a sudden, I saw him fall back."

Irvan regretted that the duel was over.

"The tire went down and Jeff [passed] under me," he said. "I turned into the corner and it didn't turn. The good Lord was watching over us and kept us from hitting a fence. But I guess he can't keep us from losing a tire."

Two weeks later, Irvan found out firsthand how dangerous it is to lose a tire. He was in Michigan, practicing for the GM Goodwrench Dealer 400. Again he lost a tire; this time, the right front one blew out while Irvan's car was traveling at high speed. The ensuing crash nearly cost Irvan his life. His subsequent return to racing is one of the most heart-warming stories in the history of the sport.

But after the race on August 6, 1994, this battle-seasoned soldier of the asphalt saluted his young conqueror—the heir apparent. "He was like any rookie," Irvan said. "He's made mistakes in the last year and a half, but there's not a guy in the garage who doesn't think he has a lot—*a lot*—of raw talent. He's already done things at an age when most of us were not even sitting in a Winston Cup car. I know I'll be racing him most of my career."

Hundreds of thousands of people were on their feet standing and cheering when Gordon's Chevrolet crossed the three-foot strip of original bricks that mark the finish line. As Gordon drove slowly down pit road toward Victory Circle, dozens of crewmen from other teams gave him high fives, raised thumbs, and victory signs.

"By God, we've got a great driver," Evernham said. "The Kid is just phenomenal."

Hendrick was probably less surprised by the victory than anyone. "I think Jeff grew up way before this [race]," he said. "But he's matured a lot this year. He's more patient. He knows when to race. He knows how to win."

Gordon finished four car-lengths ahead of Brett Bodine. Brett will be remembered for a celebrated late-race bumping incident with his brother Geoff. (This reminded some onlookers of the Allison brothers—Bobby and Donnie—who, a generation before, had often nicked each other's cars in the name of competition.) Eventually, Brett spun out Geoff, making it easier for Gordon to win.

"The only car I was worried about was that No. 7 car," he said of Geoff Bodine. "You know I saw him have his misfortune and I thought 'Well, all I got to do is be nice and smooth and ride it out from here.' "

It didn't work out that way, but Irvan's tire problem took Gordon's last serious threat from the race.

Not only did he prove he could win on the most famous race track in the world, Jeff Gordon also showed how to hide his emotions a little better. Unlike his win in Charlotte, this time he did not sit in his car crying on national television.

After crossing the finish line at the Brickyard, Jeff Gordon took not one but two victory laps. He got out of his car all smiles. "That's why I took an extra lap, so I could wipe all the tears off my face," he admitted. "I can't control my emotions at a time like this. But I don't want to be known as a crybaby all the time."

Excited as he was, Gordon made no attempt to say the Brickyard victory was the biggest of his life.

"When I won at Charlotte, that was a great thrill," he said. "I wouldn't have wanted to win my first race at any other place than Charlotte. And I wouldn't want to win my second race at any other place than here. Winning that race at Charlotte prepared us to win here. I don't think a guy who hasn't won a race could come here and win this race."

He also thought the fact that no one had any experience on the Indy racetrack gave him a better chance to win there than at any of the old tracks on the circuit.

"This was a track with no history of Winston Cup races," he said. "It's tough to race on those tracks where all these guys have been racing for so many years. Right now, we're just learning the ropes, learning the race tracks."

As he was growing up, Gordon hoped for a victory celebration at the Indianapolis Motor Speedway, but he didn't think he'd get there in a stock car. After all, it wasn't by accident his family wound up living less than a half-hour from the track. That's where he had to be to become a race car driver, they figured. Indy cars were to be his ticket to stardom.

"I didn't grow up around stock cars," Gordon said. "I grew up around open-wheeled cars, and Indy cars and all that was really a part of life. But when I got to a certain age, I realized it didn't matter where I went as long as I was racing. There wasn't any certain place that really took me away. It's just that I went looking for opportunities, and opportunities came to me in stock cars."

Although the cars he drove to victory in the Coca-Cola 600 and the Brickyard 400 gave Gordon pretty rides, only one had a pretty name. The Charlotte car was called Brooker, after his fiance.

But the Indianapolis car was named Booger, and it's now on display to the public. "Booger is headed to the Indy Museum," Evernham said later in the season. "But we've got some races to win with it first."

Firsts were on Gordon's mind that afternoon. "As bad as my memory is, I still remember Ray Harroun's name," Gordon said of the winner of the first Indianapolis 500. "I don't know what it was like back in 1911. I don't if anyone anticipated the race like they did this one. Everyone wanted to win this one."

That they did, but only The Kid was celebrating at the end. But in the wake of that party, he talked about something that would mean more than a victory at Charlotte or Indy.

"The topper of them all would be to win a Winston Cup championship," he said. "It may be out of reach this season, but we're the team of the future."

Little did he know at the time that the future was only a year away.

THE AFTERMATH

J eff Gordon wasn't even finished with his victory lap in the Brickyard 400 when the celebration began in Pittsboro. Without any planning, a parade of cars took to the streets of the town of less than a thousand people soon after Gordon saw the checkered flag at the Indianapolis Motor Speedway.

"This is probably the most exciting day anybody around here has had in years," said Terry Smith, co-owner of Smitty's Pub, where fans watched the race. "There were cheers. There were tears. It was phenomenal, just phenomenal."

"I think everybody thought he had a good shot," said Vince Posthauer, owner of the Pittsboro Pizza Shop. "The way he's been driving, being rookie of the year last year and his win at

The trophy for winning the first running of the Brickyard 400 stands at his left, but Jeff Gordon has eyes (and lips) only for his fiancée, Brooke Sealy. Gordon and the former Miss Winston Cup got married three months later.

the Coca-Cola 600, I think everybody was just hoping."

Cork and Cap Liquors had a surge in business right after the race, owner Danny Broughton said. "This place is rocking," he said that day. "They're going to burn down the town tonight, I have a feeling. The place just erupted."

Later, Jeff Gordon was almost as happy with them as they were with him. "I've heard they put banners and they're real proud of me," he said. "I'm proud to say I raced and grew up in Indiana."

The Indiana connection reminded him of the biggest thrill of his boyhood. His classmates had oohed and aahed when he showed them the autograph of four-time Indianapolis 500 winner Rick Mears that he owned. Now other school kids—and their parents—were clamoring for his autograph.

The demand for his autograph created a little problem for Gordon. He was caught between two contracts. He was supposed to sign autographs at Tri-State Speedway in Haubstadt, Indiana, where he raced sprint cars as a teen-ager. But because he had won the Brickyard 400, he had to go to Disney World the next day and serve as grand marshal of a parade.

"It's very unfortunate that Jeff was not able to make his appearance," Gordon spokesman Jimmy Johnson said of the Tri-State problem. (Johnson should not be confused with the football coach of the same name.) "But the sponsors put millions of dollars into racing. When you win the biggest race in the history of the world, you have to do what you have to do. Jeff would not do anything to hurt the Tri-State Speedway and the Indiana fans.

"I'm sure he will make it up to the fans," Johnson continued. "He volunteered to do another date at no charge. The Indiana fans are real race fans. I would certainly hope they would understand Jeff had no other choice."

A day after winning the race, Gordon was still excited. It was not hard to understand why. "I didn't sleep a wink last night," he said. "I was wide awake all night, tossing and turning and going through every moment, every lap. I'm still full of energy, so I'm still on cloud nine. I'm still very excited. It's going to take awhile for it to really sink in."

How did he celebrate in the hours after the race? A big dinner? A huge party? No, Jeff Gordon didn't want any of that. He simply wanted to spend a quiet evening with Brooke and watch the delayed local TV broadcast of the race. He wanted to see what he did to earn his $613,000.

"We didn't know what we wanted to do for dinner, so we ordered a pizza," Gordon said. "Terry Labonte was in the motel and he called me and asked what I was doing. I told him we were getting ready to eat a pizza and watch TV, and he couldn't believe it. He thought I was going to have a big party or something exciting. The excitement was winning that race. I guess Brooke and I wanted to talk about it and enjoy it with each other."

The pizzeria was very busy when Gordon's order came in and said there would be an hour and 45-minute wait. "Brooke and I were starving and we didn't know what we were going to do, " Gordon remembers. "I asked what was taking so long, and they said they 'just had that race over there at the race track.' I said, 'Does it help if I'm the winner of that race?' They said to hold on and went to get another guy. He said, 'Mr. Gordon, may I help you?' I asked if there was any way I could get a pizza before two hours. They said they'd see what they could do.

"That pizza showed up in about 25 minutes. I gave them a big tip. I felt like I had a little to spare that day."

Later, Mari George, the chairman of the track and mother of track president Tony George, invited them over her home to watch the race on TV. They had a bunch of celebrities over," Gordon recalled. "I didn't want to turn her down, but I was relaxing, watching the race."

Soon, the Gordon effect reached beyond the sport. It was felt in the Post Office. "I never knew a letter could get to me just saying Jeff Gordon, race car driver, and show up in my box," he said with a laugh.

The federal government had discovered him, and now he was the new darling of the fans. He had more people visiting him before races than ever before. "When you come to the race track, it's a little more like [Dale] Earnhardt's trailer where there's a few people waiting outside when you go in and come out," he said. "I don't know if it's hectic, but it's everything you could ever dream for or ever want."

In 1995, Gordon won races at Rockingham, Atlanta, Bristol, Daytona, Loudon, Darlington, and Dover. The number of people showing up to shake his hand, ask for an autograph, or simply watch his marvelous driving were increasing with every outing.

Later, Gordon joked that one advantage he had over the older drivers was that he had learned to lap the field while playing video games. Dale

Earnhardt and the other "old-timers" either never played video racer or had long outgrown it, whereas Gordon kept up several of his youthful habits. Of course, The Kid had actually learned to drive the hard way—on the tracks, piloting go-karts, quarter midgets, sprint cars, or whatever vehicle was available to him.

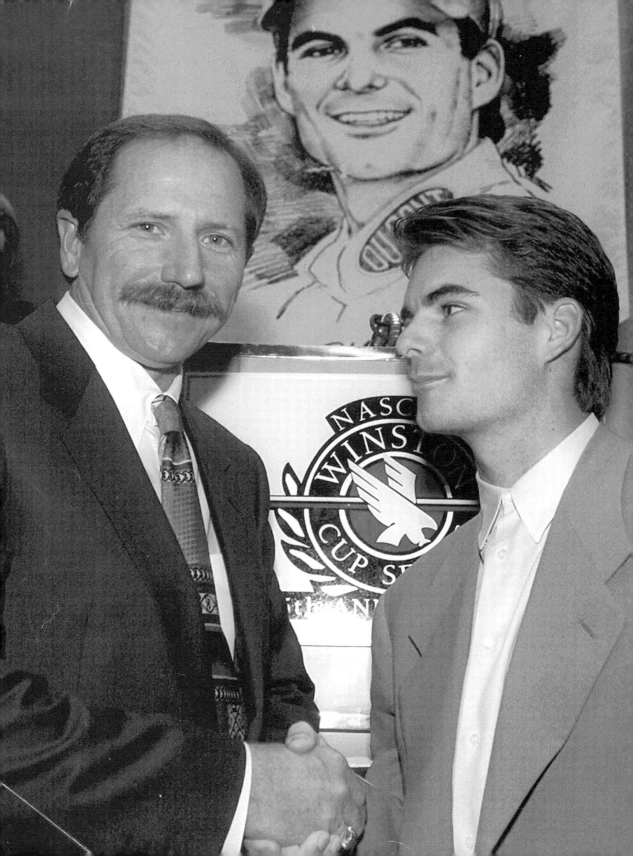

6

THE CHAMPION

Dale Earnhardt has even more nicknames than Gordon. He has been called The Intimidator, The Dominator, The Terminator, The Man In Black, Darth Vader, Ironhead, and some less complimentary things.

At the race track there are two groups of fans. Those who root for Earnhardt and those who root against him. Earnhardt fans often try to mimic him, wearing the shirts, hats, and other assorted items that he tends to favor. They dress in black, style their mustaches like that of Earnhardt and wear sunglasses similar to his trademark reflective shades. At the track, there can be as many Dale Earnhardt look-alikes as there are Presleys at an Elvis impersonators contest.

Those who root against Earnhardt often wear T-shirts imprinted with the words, "Anybody But Earnhardt."

At the news conference announcing his winning the 1995 Winston Cup, Jeff Gordon shakes hands with Dale Earnhardt, winner of seven Winston Cup titles.

Earnhardt's philosophy on the track has always been: Win at all costs. Those who don't move fast enough are nudged aside. He has bumped more than his fair share of opposing drivers, sometimes forcing them into the wall, off the track, or into dangerous spins and crashes. Fans never appreciate seeing their hero bumped by Dale Earnhardt.

Earnhardt has been the most successful stock-car racer since the legendary Richard Petty. But he has never been as beloved as "The King," who was largely responsible for the rise in popularity of stock-car racing. Indeed, Earnhardt has worked to create his image of the bad guy in the black hat, the angry gunslinger come to town to seek revenge.

Once, when asked why he ignored a black flag ordering him to stop his oil-leaking car, Earnhardt explained: "I wasn't looking for the black, I was looking for the checker."

Another time, after a brilliant drive to a runner-up finish, Earnhardt refused to accept praise for his effort. "Second ain't no good," he said.

Earnhardt is tough and gruff. He asks for no mercy on the race track and offers none. He is the genuine superstar of his time and the perhaps the most controversial driver ever.

He also happens to be one thing more, as even many of his critics will concede. Dale Earnhardt is arguably the best driver in the history of the sport. Others will argue loud and long against him because they don't like his rough driving tactics.

Earnhardt has had one major failure. He has never won the Daytona 500, the greatest stock-

car race of them all. He has tried 17 times, with all kinds of bad luck keeping him from a trip to the winner's circle. Once, he dominated the race for 499 miles. But he ran over a broken part on the track and blew a tire with one mile remaining.

Like him or not, no one will call Dale Earnhardt dull. He is the most spectacular driver on the circuit. A twist of fate—or a penalty from NASCAR—that puts him at the rear of the field, always brings excitement to crowds of 100,000 fans because most know what is to follow. One of the thrills of a Winston Cup race is to watch the black number 3 Chevrolet roar through a 42-car pack. Earnhardt is a master at finding ways to pass other drivers even if the other cars are traveling at nearly 200 miles per hour.

At times, Earnhardt must take evasive action. He has been known to get his car sideways, spin it around or cut through the grass—all without losing a position. Few ever have shown such abil-

Gordon raises dust doing a 360-spin at the start-finish line at the Atlanta Motor Speedway to celebrate his victory at the 1995 NAPA 500.

ity to handle a speeding car weighing nearly two tons.

In 1994, Earnhardt won his seventh Winston Cup title. Only Richard Petty had won that many before. No other driver had won more than three driver's championships. Many people had thought Petty's record of seven titles would never be touched. But not only had Earnhardt tied him, he had also won those titles in a shorter time span than Petty. He had won four times in the past five years, and entered the 1995 season as odds-on favorite to win his eighth championship. His next Winston Cup title would be his eighth, one more than the legendary Richard Petty.

Then along came Jeff Gordon.

The Kid dominated the circuit for much of the season.

But titles are not easily won. And old champions don't go quietly. Earnhardt certainly didn't.

On the July Fourth weekend in 1995, Gordon won the Pepsi 400. That gave him victories at Indianapolis, Charlotte and Daytona, the three great American race tracks. If he had announced his retirement that day, his career would already have been a success.

But anyone thinking along those lines would have missed the larger story. One can never be really sure when or where a torch is passed, but after it happens, everyone recognizes it.

"I don't know if it's been passed or not," one veteran sports writer told another after Gordon was forced to drive more than 100 miles on two worn tires on the way to a win in July at Loudon, New Hampshire. "But it's certainly in transit."

It may have passed from Earnhardt to Gordon the following week at Pocono International Raceway. On that hot Sunday afternoon, virtually all the Chevrolets were beaten badly by the Fords. Thunderbirds took eight of the first nine positions. On days such as those, Earnhardt usually finds a way to survive—even thrive. But not in Miller Genuine Draft 500.

"Same car, same junk," Earnhardt said after a 20th-place finish left him 164 points behind Gordon in the standings. "I'm so disgusted and frustrated and aggravated."

Earnhardt and Chevy aces Sterling Marlin and Terry Labonte were no factor.

But one Chevy driver flourished. "We did not have a second-place car all day long," Gordon said after an Earnhardt-like effort carried his balky Chevrolet within 80 feet of his third straight victory.

Gordon waves to fans outside the Waldorf-Astoria Hotel in New York City after the dinner honoring his Winston Cup championship.

He was only five car-lengths behind the Thunderbird of Dale Jarrett when the checkered flag waved. After a valiant effort, Gordon finished second.

With an explanation he could have borrowed from Earnhardt, Gordon blamed himself for not winning. "We had a two-tire stop and I totally

Race car legend Richard Petty (left) talks with a race car legend in the making, Jeff Gordon (right) in the garage area at the North Carolina Motor Speedway.

forgot about it," he said. "I was just sitting there taking a drink. They dropped the jack and I stalled it."

A month earlier, at the same race track, a poorly executed shift cost him an almost-certain victory and 60 points. In other years, that type of error would have been hard to forget. But in 1995, Gordon overcame errors of inexperience and rode his team's "refuse-to-lose" approach to a commanding lead in Winston Cup points by mid-season.

"They had to fight real hard to get us back up there," he said after the crew overcame his pit-road lapse at Pocono. "So, this one's for the team."

A week earlier, Gordon credited crew chief Ray Evernham's strategy for the victory at New Hampshire International Speedway. The closest Gordon will come to claiming responsibility for winning is, "I drove my heart out."

"If anything, I drove too hard," he said after nearly stealing the spotlight from the Fords at Pocono.

Still, he was on his way, and people were starting to notice. Perhaps the first to realize how great Gordon could be was three-time Winston Cup champion Darrell Waltrip. He compared Gordon to a great pitcher, saying you had to get to him early. "Once he gets rolling, that boy will be hard to beat," Waltrip said.

Gordon was rolling, and didn't stop until he had season-bests of seven victories and eight poles.

If so, Waltrip might have several more moments to remember. Still, he'll never forget what he saw on March 24, 1995.

Waltrip has won 84 races, tying him for third on the NASCAR career list, so he is not easily impressed. But when Gordon became the only driver ever to qualify at difficult Darlington at a speed in excess of 170 miles per hour, even "Ol' DW" was stunned.

Watching Gordon attack the treacherous old track as no one ever had, Waltrip thought about some of the late greats of racing. "When Gordon ran what he did, Curtis Turner, Fireball Roberts, Joe Weatherly, all them guys up in heaven said, 'I'm glad I ain't running Darlington this weekend.' "

It was no fluke. Gordon was awesome, and looked like a sure winner. But he and Bobby Labonte crashed late in the race.

The kiss at the winner's celebration in the TranSouth 400 went to Marlin. Visibly, all Gordon had to show for his effort was a badly broken race car.

Emotionally, the scars ran deeper. For perhaps the only time all season there was a bit of doubt. "I guess the ego around the garage area is that you're not a real race car driver until you've won at Darlington," he said. "I believe that as much as anybody else."

He remedied that six months later, winning the coveted Southern 500 at Darlington.

At the end of the season, Earnhardt made an amazing run at the championship. Gordon's 305-point lead was reduced to 34 when Earnhardt won the last of the 31 races. But it wasn't quite enough.

"He'll be up there drinking that milk at the front table," Earnhardt said of Gordon that November day in Atlanta.

A month later, Gordon showed up in New York to collect his Winston Cup check for $1.3 million. He didn't forget Earnhardt's quip. "Dale," he said, raising a champagne glass for all to see as he saluted a worthy but beaten foe.

Then Gordon downed its contents. It may have been the first milk toast in the history of the famed Waldorf Astoria Hotel.

"I see why this guy wants to do it so many times." Gordon said. "There are lots of things to be happy about, and that's a lot of money."

Indeed. Including postseason bonuses, he earned a record $4,347,343 in 1995. His racing purses totaled $2,430,460, which led the Winston Cup circuit.

Earnhardt, whose 68 career victories is sixth on the all-time list, is hardly ready to concede that Gordon is now the best driver on the track. "I don't know what people are expecting out of him, if he's going to be greater than sliced bread or what," the Intimidator said. "I don't think he's going to be a better driver than Richard Petty was. Winning one championship doesn't make him the greatest driver in the world. He's a good driver, but he's got a long way to go to win 200-plus races and seven or eight championships."

During his championship run, Gordon would not permit talk of a possible series title to interfere with the main thrust of the team. "We don't think about championship, we don't talk about championship," he said midway through the season. "We just get ready for the next race."

Gordon was only 24 when he accepted the trophy that meant for at least a year he was the greatest stock car driver on the earth and the second-youngest Winston Cup champion ever. Bill Rexford was 23 when he won in 1950. Earnhardt was 29 when he won his first title in 1980. →Was a rookie in 79!

Before the 1995 season had ended, Earnhardt and Gordon were together on boxes of Kelloggs' Frosted Mini-Wheats, billed as "The Champ" and "The Kid."

When the checkered flag fell for the last time, Gordon was both.

In 1996, Gordon had another wonderful year. For several months, he led in the Winston Cup championship, and experts were predicting another title for the young racer. But Terry Labonte won a string of races right at the end of the season, and in one of the tightest finishes in history, eked out his second driving championship. (He had also won one in 1984.)

In 1997, Gordon got off to a flying start by winning the Daytona 500.

Early in the race, he pitted when he thought he had a flat tire and told his crew chief, "I've just cost us the race." But some aggressive driving brought him back to the front, and when Dale Earnhardt crashed twice, including once near the end of the race, Gordon got to cruise to the finish line under the yellow flag. At age 25, Gordon became the youngest driver ever to win Daytona.

While the Daytona 500 was the first race and first win for Jeff in the 1997 season, there were other victories just as sweet. By winning the Winston Million, a series of three of the most anticipated NASCAR events (the Daytona 500, Coca-Cola 600, and Southern 500), Jeff joined Bill Elliot as the only drivers to accomplish the feat since its conception in 1985. In total, Gordon won 10 of his 32 races in 1997, won over $6.5 million, and took home his second Winston Cup.

Jeff is making a difference on and off the track. Despite his busy schedule, he gives back to the community through charity involvement with Easter Seals, the Make-A-Wish Foundation, which grants wishes to terminally ill children, and the Leukemia Society of America. His car owner, Rick Hendrick, is currently fighting a form of leukemia and his crew chief, Ray Evernham's son, was also diagnosed with the disease.

Having made Winston Cup history in his seven-year racing career, he recently joined the list of NASCAR's Top 20 winningest drivers. Already the equal of many veteran drivers, Jeff Gordon is expected to be a force in the racing world for years to come.

STATISTICS

Year	Races	Wins	Top 5 Finishes	Top 10 Finishes	Money Won
1992	1	0	0	0	$6,285
1993	30	0	7	11	$765,168
1994	31	2	7	14	$1,779,523
1995	31	7	17	23	$4,347,343
1996	31	10	21	24	$3,428,485
1997	32	10	22	23	$6,501,227
Career	156	29	74	95	$16,828,031

13
7
49
+ 3
52 - 2000'
+ 14 - 2001'

JEFF GORDON
A CHRONOLOGY

1971   Born on August 4, in Vallejo, California.

1979   Wins first national championship, in quarter midget cars.

1981   Repeats as quarter midget national champion.

1985   Drives sprint cars in Indiana and on the winter circuit in Florida.

1989   Wins USAC midgets championship.

1991   Named Grand National Rookie of the Year driving stock cars.

1992   Signs with Rick Hendrick; wins 11 Busch poles and three races.

1993   Becomes youngest driver ever to win a Daytona qualifier; wins Rookie-of-the-Year honors on the Winston Cup circuit.

1994   Wins Coca-Cola 600, his first Winston Cup race; marries Brooke Sealy, winner of the 1993 Miss Winston beauty pageant; wins inaugural Brickyard 400.

1995   Wins seven races and a record $4,347,343 en route to becoming second-youngest driver ever to win a Winston Cup championship.

1996   Finishes second in Winston Cup competition.

1997   Becomes youngest driver ever to win the Daytona 500; winner of the inaugural California 500; winner of the Winston Million; wins second Winston Cup championship; becomes first driver to post $6 million in earnings for a season.

SUGGESTIONS FOR FURTHER READING

Hinton, Ed. "On the Fast Track." *Sports Illustrated*, April 24, 1995.

Vogelin, Rick. "The Natural." *Sport Magazine*, February, 1995.

ABOUT THE AUTHOR

Dick Brinster has been covering stock car racing since 1980 as a sports writer for the Associated Press. He lives in New Jersey.

INDEX